# Owl in the Cedar Tree

# Owl in the Cedar Tree

By NATACHEE SCOTT MOMADAY

Illustrated by DON PERCEVAL

University of Nebraska Press
Lincoln and London

First Bison Book printing: 1992
Most recent printing indicated by the last digit below:
10   9   8   7   6   5   4   3   2   1

Library of Congress Cataloging-in-Publication Data
Momaday, Natachee Scott.
Owl in the cedar tree / by Natachee Scott Momaday; illustrated by Don
Perceval.
p.   cm.
Originally published: Boston: Ginn, 1965.
Summary: A Navaho boy with a secret wish is torn by conflicting cultures.
ISBN 0-8032-8184-6 (pa)
1. Navajo Indians—Juvenile fiction.  [1. Navajo Indians—Fiction.
2. Indians of North America—Fiction.]   I. Perceval, Don Louis, ill.
II. Title.
PZ7.M73550w   1965b
[Fic]—dc20
91-41866   CIP
AC

Reprinted by arrangement with Natachee Scott Momaday

The University of Nebraska Press is grateful to Edith Perceval for per-
mission to reproduce, in black and white for this Bison Book edition, the
illustrations of her husband, Don Perceval.

∞

To Cael and Jill

# CONTENTS

| CHAPTER | | PAGE |
|---|---|---|
| ONE | Haske, a Navaho Boy | 1 |
| TWO | Haske's Home | 5 |
| THREE | Cry of the Owl | 10 |
| FOUR | Old Grandfather | 16 |
| FIVE | The Bear | 25 |
| SIX | A Warrior Returns | 31 |
| SEVEN | A Hitchhiker Is Picked Up | 38 |
| EIGHT | Navaho Sing | 45 |
| NINE | A Paper from Washington | 51 |
| TEN | Back to School | 62 |
| ELEVEN | The Storm | 67 |
| TWELVE | The Hunt | 71 |
| THIRTEEN | Best of the Old, Best of the New | 77 |
| FOURTEEN | A Christmas Present | 85 |
| FIFTEEN | A Beautiful Way to Go | 89 |
| SIXTEEN | The Owl's Message | 97 |
| SEVENTEEN | Haske Sings the Happiness Song | 107 |

# CHAPTER ONE

# Haske, a Navaho Boy

HASKE lay flat on his stomach and drew a picture in the golden sand. His brown finger moved slowly as he traced the outline of a horse. Haske was a Navaho boy and all Navaho boys love horses, but Haske loved one horse more than all others. He loved Night Wind, the black horse which belonged to Store Sitter, the trader.

No one knew that Haske loved Night Wind so much. His father, Night Singer, did not know. His mother, Riding Woman, did not know. Even Desbah, his little sister, did not know about his love for the beautiful black horse. They did not know because Haske did not like to talk about it. When a boy wants something as much as Haske wanted the black horse, it hurts to talk about it. So he told no one. He just kept the secret in his heart.

Whenever he went to the Trading Post, he would slip around to the corral, stroke Night Wind's head, and whisper, "I wish we could always be together. We would find beautiful places to visit. We would feel the rain in our faces as we raced across the desert. We would be as brothers." The horse would lay his warm nose, which felt like velvet, against Haske's shoulder, toss his head and whinny softly.

Haske sat back on his heels and viewed the picture he had made. He liked to draw. During the long days while the sheep grazed among the clumps of desert grass, Haske saw beauty in the shapes about him. He loved the tinted mesas, the desert flowers, and the darkly brooding mountains. Sometimes a lizard or a horned toad stopped to rest on a rock nearby. Then Haske would make a sand drawing of the little reptile. He always wished that he might take home the pictures he made and show them to Desbah. He wished that he had a pencil and paper on which to draw. He thought about the time he had gone to school for a while, remembering the

paper and pencils there. His fingers fairly throbbed with the desire to draw. The feeling was so strong it was like being hungry all the time. He could not help drawing any more than he could help loving the black horse.

Haske looked at the shadows which were growing long. They reached like fingers across the desert. The sun was very low. Slowly he erased the picture of the black horse as his hands moved lovingly over the sand. Then he stood up and whistled to his dogs, Gray Eyes and Ute. It was time to go home.

The dogs were trained to guard the sheep and to help drive them. They were good dogs and knew how to protect the family as well as the sheep. At Haske's whistle they began turning the sheep toward home. When a lamb or an old sheep lagged behind, the dogs barked and gently nudged it forward. Gray Eyes and Ute were happy to be going home. They knew the family's supper would be shared with them.

# CHAPTER TWO

# Haske's Home

HASKE's home was called a hogan. His father had built it of logs and earth. The door looked eastward across miles of golden sand. On the western side, nearby, were beautiful mountains. There tall pine trees grew. There, too, were springs of clear cold water, and purple shadows which cooled the earth.

Inside the round log house there were no tables or chairs. There were no beds or carpets. There was not even a stove. The floor was the good hard earth. Each morning Riding Woman swept it clean. In the center of the floor was a small fire pit where fires were built for cooking. In winter the fire kept the family warm.

Haske's bed was of soft fluffy sheepskins which were spread on the floor at night. Each member of the family had his own sheepskin bed and a bright warm blanket. Early each morning the fluffy beds, together with the blankets, were rolled up neatly and placed against the walls. They were used as seats during the day.

Against the walls, hanging from pegs, were pots for cooking and beautiful strings of turquoise beads, the color of the sky. All of the family's clothing was folded neatly and kept in a box against the wall. Most Navaho homes are like Haske's.

Haske was never lonely. On the desert he played with horned toads, lizards, and prairie dogs. In the mountains he played with chipmunks and squirrels. He watched birds and listened to their songs.

Gray Eyes and Ute were his constant companions. They worked and played together. When they were not herding his mother's sheep, they liked to hunt. Haske loved all animals and did not want to see them killed. Only when there was hunger in his mother's hogan and Desbah cried for food would he kill an animal.

During the long winter months food was scarce. There were no prickly pears on the desert and no fat pine nuts in the mountains. All of the stored corn was used up long before winter was over. In winter, more than any other time, they all looked to Riding Woman, the mother. The sheep belonged to her, and she used the wool to weave into rugs. These she sold or traded for food and clothing at the Trading Post. It took weeks, sometimes months, to weave a rug. She worked very hard, but each winter there was little food. Often the family went hungry.

In winter the big loom on which Riding Woman wove her rugs was brought into the house. The bench and the tools for making jewelry were placed near the fire pit. Here Night Singer sometimes worked as a silversmith, making silver rings, bracelets, and necklaces when he could afford to buy blocks of silver. In winter, too, he hauled fire wood from the mountains and made long trips to bring water from the spring for home use. He often went hunting for game so the family might have meat.

When spring came, Night Singer planted corn, squash, and melons in a small field near the hogan. He had no plow or farm machinery, so he simply dug holes in the earth with a pointed stick. Then he dropped in the seeds, and with his feet tramped the earth tightly down over them. Springtime was also sheep-shearing time.

During the hot dry months of summer, water had to be hauled several miles to the thirsty plants. Wood for cooking must still be brought from the mountains, and weeds must be pulled from around the field plants so that the crops might grow and mature. Later the crops would be harvested and hauled to the house. There they would be dried and stored away to be used very sparingly and made to last as long as possible.

A cedar tree stood before the hogan door, and here the family cooked and ate in summer. In hot weather Riding Woman set her loom under the cedar tree. While she worked in the cool shade, Desbah played nearby.

Near the hogan were the corrals where the sheep slept at night. Beside the corrals was a shed where the family wagon was kept and where the two horses were fed. One horse belonged to Riding Woman. She was a great horse-woman and had ridden in many Navaho races. She was a far better rider than most men, and that is why she was called Riding Woman. The other horse belonged to Night Singer. Whenever he had been away all day and came home late at night, he sang the Navaho Riding Song so the family would know he was coming home. He had a beautiful voice.

Haske would not have traded his home for any other in all the world.

# CHAPTER THREE

# Cry of the Owl

ONE MORNING in August Haske awoke before dawn. He had been dreaming of riding the black horse, Night Wind. He often dreamed of the horse because he loved him so, but always he awoke and knew that Night Wind belonged to Store Sitter.

Haske stared into the darkness and wondered why he had awakened. Everything was still and quiet. He listened to the soft breathing of his mother, his father, and his little sister. He felt all the stillness of the desert. He felt all the loneliness of the night. Dawn Woman, who brings the daylight, had not yet come across the desert.

Suddenly he heard a noise, the same noise which had awakened him. It was the hoot of an owl, and it sounded near the door!

Haske shivered as he remembered some of the tales the old people told of the owl. They said, "The owl always brings bad news. If an owl cries three times near your home, something very bad will happen." Night Singer and Riding Woman did not believe these things. They said such beliefs were superstition. But who could be sure?

Haske quietly crawled to the door. The owl had already spoken twice. It must not speak again.

Outside, he felt in the darkness for a pebble. His hand closed around a small round stone. Before he could throw the stone, he heard the rustling of great wings, and the tree shook as the owl flew away. Haske was glad he had not thrown the stone. He might have killed the owl! Even though owls bring messages of sickness and evil, they are respected for their great wisdom. No one wants to kill an owl.

After that, Haske did not feel like sleeping. He sat down on the cool earth and leaned back against his mother's hogan. For a while he sat in the darkness and thought about many things. After a while he saw Dawn Woman coming silently across the desert. She was bringing with her the first faint light of the day.

He said very softly, speaking only to the Dawn
Woman and within himself:

"Dawn Woman, beautiful, beautiful,
You come to me, you come to me,
Across the desert,
Over the mountains,
Weaving a blanket of light."

He heard the sheep moving in the corral. Gray
Eyes and Ute came and sat beside him with ears
pointed and alert. Haske watched the light in the
East grow brighter, and suddenly the rim of the sun
peeped over the horizon. Now was the time to sing
the Sunrise Song, the song Night Singer had taught

him and given him for his own greeting to the sun.
He lifted his arms toward the rising sun and sang:

> "Arise! Arise!
> From the East he comes,
> In the East his eyes are upon me.
> Arrows fly from his bow,
> Arrows of golden light, nizhoni, nizhoni!
> They bring happiness,
> They bring long life,
> They bring holiness.
> Arise!  Arise in beauty!"

Haske dropped his arms and stroked the dogs.  He
wished that they might talk.  He wondered if they,

too, had been afraid of the owl. Perhaps they understood what the owl had said.

Old Grandfather had told him that once there was a time when dogs spoke the Navaho language. But something had happened long ago and after that dogs and people could not communicate. To Haske's disappointment Old Grandfather had forgotten what had happened.

Riding Woman came out of the hogan and went to the wash bench by the cedar tree. She dipped water from a barrel nearby and washed her face and hands.

She said to Haske, "Why is my son up so early this morning?"

He answered, "I have seen the Dawn Woman come to my mother's hogan." That is all he said. He did not want to tell her about the owl.

Night Singer came next to the wash bench. He washed his face and hands and then sat down by Haske. The mountaintops were turning rosy pink and the desert floor was turquoise blue. The world was awakening.

"I liked your Sunrise Song," he said to Haske. "I, too, feel like singing praises to the new light of day."

His voice was strong and beautiful as he lifted his arms toward the rising sun and sang:

> "The curtain of daylight is hanging,
>     It is hanging.
> It is hanging from the land of day,
>     It is hanging.
> Before me as it dawns,
>     It is hanging.
> Behind me as it dawns,
>     It is hanging.
> Before me in beauty,
>     It is hanging.
> Behind me in beauty,
>     It is hanging.
> The curtain of light is hanging."

It was good to sit here in the early morning and listen to his father's voice. It was good to see beauty all about him and to sing thanks to the gods of light. It was also good to smell coffee boiling in the tin pot and to hear his mother moving about as she cooked breakfast. Desbah was still asleep on her blanket. But Haske could not forget the owl.

Old Grandfather believed the owl was a messenger of evil tidings. He understood such things, and Haske wished that the wise old man were here with him now. He needed to ask some questions.

# CHAPTER FOUR

# Old Grandfather

AFTER BREAKFAST Haske took the sheep to the mountains. The grass there was good. Gray Eyes and Ute went along to help herd the sheep. Gray Eyes was a mother dog. She liked to stay near Haske. Ute was a hunter and a fighter. He liked to run ahead and look for adventure.

When they reached the foothills, they found tall grass and a spring of water. The sheep began eating eagerly. Haske climbed a little higher and sat down on soft pine needles. Here he could see the sheep below him. Here, too, he could see far across the desert beyond his home. Both dogs came to sit beside him, but they were alert. They kept their eyes on the sheep grazing below and their ears pointed up and listening.

Haske watched a blue jay hop among the branches of a pine tree. Far above, an eagle swooped after a small bird. How Haske wished he had paper and a pencil!

Suddenly Ute growled. Gray Eyes sniffed the air and got up to move nearer the sheep. Haske looked and at last saw the tiny figure of a man moving slowly toward them across the desert.

He spoke to the dogs, "You have strong ears and eyes. You have strong noses too."

Haske continued to watch for a while, until the figure came nearer and grew larger. Then he saw it was an old man who walked with the aid of a stick. As the old man began to climb the slope below them, Haske smiled and said to the dogs, "That is my Old Grandfather! Do your ears and eyes and noses forget so quickly?"

By Old Grandfather, Haske meant his great-grandfather. The old man was almost blind and very frail. He was a kind old man who always talked of things which happened long ago. He never thought

of things as they are now, but always as they used to be. Haske jumped up and ran down the mountain to meet him.

"Good morning, Old Grandfather," Haske said and took his arm to help him up the mountain.

"Good morning, my grandson. I am glad to find you here," answered the old man. "I came because I used to live up here many years ago."

Haske saw a tin cup tied to the old man's belt. It was for water when he became thirsty. The cup was his very own. It was the only piece of property the old man had. His relatives gave him cast-off clothing once in a while, but he did not feel that the clothing was really his own. Haske was very sorry for his Old Grandfather.

Some of his relatives did not treat the old man kindly. They were afraid that he might die in their hogan. They believed that when a person dies in a hogan it must be burned. This is an old Navaho superstition. Old Grandfather believed it too. He had burned his hogan when his wife died many years ago. He understood how many of his relatives felt, and he did not want to cause them any trouble. So he wandered around most of the time.

Night Singer and Riding Woman did not believe in this old custom. They had each attended a Government Boarding School when they were young and had lived away from their people. They had learned that people must change with the changing times. They knew that much of their way of life was good, and they were proud of being Navaho. But they would not hold to the old superstitions.

When Haske had helped Old Grandfather to sit down under a tall pine tree, he said, "Now, I shall bring you cold water from the spring. Then we shall have some lunch."

They ate the fried bread and cold mutton which Haske had brought from home. Gray Eyes and Ute had a share of the lunch too.

Haske hoped Old Grandfather would tell him a story, and waited for the old man to speak. Old Grandfather sat with his back against the tree. His eyes were closed. Finally he said:

"My grandson, it is good here. The mountains are the home of the Cloud People and the Rain Gods. They watch over our people. The mountains are good to us. They give us water. They give us logs for our hogans. They give us food and wood for our fires. Long ago, when I was a young man, I lived high up in these mountains. I was strong and happy then. Someday you must build your hogan here."

Haske answered, "Yes, Old Grandfather, some-day, I shall build my hogan here."

The old man sat very still for a long time. Haske wondered if he were sleeping, but finally he began to talk again:

"Once when I lived up here, some Plains Indians came to raid us. They were Kiowas and Comanches. They wanted to fight, and steal our horses. The Navahos had heard that they were coming, and we were ready for them." The old man paused and smiled. "Yes, we were ready for them that time.

Those buffalo eaters are good riders but not so good as the Navahos. Many of our young men met them head-on down there on the desert. They fought with bows and arrows, with lances, and even with bare hands. Many of them died that day. Then we came up from behind and drove them up here. Some of our men had gone around the mountain and were waiting for them! When they were halfway up the mountain, our men charged down upon them. They were trapped! They did not know which way to go. You should have heard the noise."

The old man pointed to a great bluff on the side of the mountain. "That is where we drove them off. Right off that high bluff. Some of the horses turned over in the air twice before they struck the ground below. When we rode down the trail to look at them, all the Comanches and Kiowas were dead. Most of their fine horses were dead too. My grandson, you should have been here in those days."

Haske thought about it. He thought to himself, "No, I am glad I did not see that. I would not like to see men and horses killed." But to Old Grandfather he answered respectfully, "You were a brave warrior. Our people defended themselves well."

Suddenly Ute sprang up and barked. Gray Eyes sniffed and growled. Haske stood up and looked about him. Old Grandfather also tried to see what was wrong, but his eyes were very old and he could not see well.

Then it happened! All in an instant the sheep began to run. They cried in a frightened way as they gathered speed, heading straight for the edge of the high bluff. If they were not turned, they would all be killed. The dogs! Where were they? But the dogs seemed to have forgotten the sheep. They were even running the other way, barking and yelping savagely.

Haske thought first of his mother's sheep. They must not come to harm. He called the dogs sharply. They turned and came back. Then with the dogs he sped after the sheep. Ute and Gray Eyes soon left the boy far behind, still Haske ran on and on. He could hear them far ahead barking as they tried to turn the sheep. By the time he caught up with them, he was gasping for breath. But there they were, the sheep huddled together and the dogs standing guard. Haske sat down and tried to breathe more slowly.

"My dogs," he said, "what wonderful friends you are! My mother's sheep might have run off the bluff like the Kiowas and the Comanches. You saved them and I shall tell my mother about your fine work today. She will feed you well this night."

# CHAPTER FIVE

# The Bear

SLOWLY HASKE and the dogs started herding the sheep toward the place where they had left Old Grandfather. The sheep led the way. Haske and the dogs followed. Suddenly the sheep whirled and started back the way they had come. Some of them almost ran over Haske. Others split to right or left of him. They ran for their very lives. The dogs leaped straight ahead, yelping. Stunned at the quick change in dogs and sheep, Haske could only stand frozen to the spot. Then he saw what had caused all the trouble. The dogs were pursuing a great brown bear. As they closed in on the bear, it turned to defend itself. A second later Haske saw Old Grandfather. He was lying on the ground. There was blood on his face and shirt.

The boy forgot about the sheep. He forgot about the dogs. Even for a moment he forgot about the bear. He ran to the old man and knelt beside him calling his name, "Old Grandfather, Old Grandfather, what happened? Speak to your grandson." But the old man did not speak.

Far above him Haske heard the yelps of the dogs and the crashing of underbrush. The sheep were gone. Haske was frightened. This had never happened to him before, and he did not know what to do. There were no hogans nearby. No one would hear him if he called for help. Whatever was to be done, he must do it all by himself. As soon as he realized this, he was no longer frightened. He must think wisely, act quickly, and do all he could possibly do to help.

Haske tore open Old Grandfather's shirt. He saw the long wound bleeding across the thin chest. He put his hand over the old man's heart and felt a faint beating. This gave him hope, for he knew that Old Grandfather was still alive. Quickly he took the old man's tin cup and ran to the spring for water.

After he had washed the blood from Old Grandfather's face, he saw deep scratches on his face and forehead. It was then that he remembered the owl! These things which had happened were foretold by the owl. Haske wondered why owls always brought bad messages. Did they never bring good news to the people? He thought about the black horse, Night Wind. If only the horse were with him now, he could race for help! He could even put Old Grandfather on Night Wind's back, and such a horse could carry them both safely home. But he did not have the black horse. He was alone, and everything depended upon him now.

While he wondered what to do, all at once there came to him from far above in the mountains a man's voice singing a Navaho song. Haske stood up and shouted for help. He shouted again and again. At last he got an answering shout.

In a little while, a thin man riding a pinto horse came toward him through the trees. It was Hosteen Yazzie who lived on the other side of the mountain. Hosteen Yazzie pushed back his cowboy hat and sprang to the ground. He knelt beside Old Grandfather and looked at him closely. He asked Haske what had happened. When he heard the story, he shook his head. Haske held the pinto's bridle while

the old man was gently lifted into the saddle. Then
Hosteen Yazzie jumped up behind him and rode
down the mountain. He held Old Grandfather in
front of him as he would have held a small child.

Haske called the dogs, but neither came. He started out alone to search for his mother's sheep. He walked and walked. The sun moved overhead and the shadows grew long. Just before dark he came to a little box canyon. Here, in the shadow of the canyon walls, he found the sheep huddled together and still frightened.

Haske counted them. Thirty-nine! They were all there. He was glad that the bear had not killed one. He could thank Gray Eyes and Ute for that.

When Haske and the sheep reached home, it was quite dark. Riding Woman helped him drive them into the corral. As they walked to the hogan together, his mother said, "You have done a good thing in finding help for Old Grandfather. You also brought the sheep safely home. I am proud of you, my son."

Inside the hogan Night Singer and Hosteen Yazzie sat against the wall smoking and talking. On a blanket near them lay Old Grandfather. Desbah was crying because the old man was hurt.

Everyone except Haske had eaten supper. Riding Woman gave him some good warm bread and mutton stew. While he ate supper, he listened to his father talking with Hosteen Yazzie.

Night Singer said, "Tomorrow morning I shall go to see the Medicine Man and ask him to hold a curing ceremony over Old Grandfather."

Hosteen Yazzie answered, "I will help you. I shall ride to many of the hogans and tell the people about the Sing and ask them to come here."

Then the two men talked of the bear. Hosteen Yazzie said, "I have never before heard of a bear hurting anyone. Bears are brave animals. They act and think like a man, but this was a bad thing for a bear to do. To strike an old man who is almost blind is a cowardly act! Maybe something was wrong with that bear."

Haske was very tired. After he had finished eating, he rolled out his sheepskin bed and lay down. He tried to listen to the stories the men were telling, but in spite of himself his eyes closed and he fell asleep.

He dreamed that he rode the black horse, Night Wind, through a canyon where strange Indians shot arrows at them. But he was not afraid because Night Wind ran faster than the arrows flew.

# CHAPTER SIX

# A Warrior Returns

NEXT MORNING Haske awoke and stretched his legs. He looked about him. Riding Woman sat on the floor holding a cup to Old Grandfather's lips. The old man was sitting up. He was better! Haske spoke to him and asked how he felt.

"I'm much better, thank you. But I'm sorry for making so much trouble," answered Old Grandfather.

Before Haske could speak, Riding Woman said, "You must not feel that way, please. We are glad that you are with us. We want to take care of you."

Haske went outside to wash. The morning air was cool. Desbah was sitting by the outdoor campfire eating her breakfast. There was hot green-corn bread and coffee. Oh! how Haske did like green-corn bread. It was made of young green corn, ground coarsely and mixed with green onions. After he had washed, Haske helped himself. But before he could take a bite, he heard a whimper and looked quickly around.

Ute had come home. Ute, the warrior! The big dog was watching him and asking for attention. Haske went to him, speaking softly, and noticed that Ute had some bad cuts on his side. He looked next for Gray Eyes but did not see her. He hoped the bear had not killed her. Gently he stroked Ute and gave him the green-corn bread.

Riding Woman came out of the hogan, smiling. She handed Haske another piece of bread and said, "Old Grandfather will be well again. But his wounds are bad and he must have care. Your father has gone for the Medicine Man."

Haske knew that today would be busy and that many things would have to be done before the ceremony. Riding Woman must butcher a sheep so there would be plenty of meat. Green corn must be gathered from the field. The hogan must be cleaned and made neat, for the Medicine Man would need space to perform the ceremony.

Hosteen Yazzie had ridden off at sunrise to invite people to the Sing.

Haske and Desbah went to the field for corn. They were worried about Gray Eyes. She was gentle and did not enjoy fighting. She fought only when she had to and when she felt it a duty. Once when a strange man had come to their home, Gray Eyes had not let the man go near Desbah. When he had tried to pick her up in his arms, Gray Eyes had sprung upon him. She loved the family very much. Now maybe she was lying dead up on the mountain. Or maybe she was hurt and crying for help.

As Haske and Desbah walked along the path to the cornfield, they were thinking of Gray Eyes. But they did not want to talk about her. Navaho people believe that if you speak of bad things, bad things will happen. They did not want to put into words the fear in their hearts, so they said nothing.

About mid-afternoon Night Singer came home. One of his uncles, Many Goats, came with him. By this time Riding Woman had finished butchering the sheep and cleaning house.

Night Singer and Many Goats hitched the horses to the wagon and put two large barrels in the wagon-bed. Then they drove to the spring which was up in the mountains several miles away. There they filled the barrels with cool spring water for home use.

While Haske was husking the corn which he and Desbah had brought from the field, he saw a horse and rider approaching. He jumped to his feet and rubbed his eyes. Surely he was dreaming! He looked again and sure enough it was Night Wind. Store Sitter was riding him right up to the hogan.

"Yah-te-heh," said the man as he got off the horse.

Haske said, "Good afternoon."

This was a joke between them. Store Sitter was polite and spoke to Haske in the Navaho language. In return, Haske was just as polite and answered in the white man's language.

Riding Woman came out of the hogan and shook hands with the visitor. She invited him in to see Old Grandfather. After a few minutes Store Sitter came to the door and called Haske.

"Take my horse and ride to the Trading Post. Give this note to my wife, and she will send medicine for the Old One. Now ride fast and hurry back, but mind you! Don't spill the medicine."

Haske put the note in his pocket and swung up onto Night Wind's back. His feet did not reach the saddle's stirrups, but he lifted the reins and the black horse broke into a gallop.

All the way to the Trading Post and home again, Haske spoke tenderly to Night Wind. The black horse laid back his ears to catch every word, but not once did he slow down. When they reached home, the bottle of medicine was safe. Haske hurried into the hogan and gave it to Store Sitter. When he came out, he held something clutched tightly in his hand. It was sugar for Night Wind.

# CHAPTER SEVEN

# A Hitchhiker Is Picked Up

RIDING WOMAN was cooking supper over the campfire. Desbah was trying to help her. Ute lay nearby enjoying the good smell of food.

Old Grandfather lay on a bright new blanket under a shelter of brush. The medicine which Store Sitter had put on the wounds made the old man feel better. Haske went over and sat down beside him.

"How do you feel?" he asked.

Old Grandfather smiled faintly as he replied, "I am going to be all right, my grandson." He stopped and thought a moment, then added, "You saved my life, but now you are in great danger. You should have left me there on the mountain."

Haske's eyes popped wide open. He wondered if the old man's fever was making him talk like this.

"But Old Grandfather!" he cried. "I would never leave you on the mountain, sick and hurt. How can you say such things? And what do you mean when you say I am in great danger?"

Haske moved nearer so he would not miss a word spoken. Old Grandfather slowly shook his head and frowned.

"It is a shame," he said, "that your father does not tell you the old truths which the Ancients taught us. How can you protect yourself if you do not know these things?"

Haske looked around to see if his mother had heard the old man's words, but she and Desbah had gone into the house.

The old man continued: "Most bears are not bad. An ordinary bear will run away before he will fight a man. He just wants to be left alone. The spirits of our ancestors sometimes live in bears. That is why our people will never kill a bear or eat bear meat. But sometimes an evil spirit enters into a bear, making him mean and dangerous. An evil spirit made the bear attack me. Now that you saved me, it will try to harm you, my grandson." The old man then closed his eyes and went to sleep.

Haske sat in deep thought. He remembered the words of Hosteen Yazzie. Maybe something *was* wrong with that bear. Did Hosteen Yazzie know the truths which the Ancients had taught the people? And did his father also know these things?

Haske knew that Navaho people do not like to kill bears and that they never eat bear meat. A bear may be killed only when he attacks a person. And never is the meat used for food. Haske had never thought much about the reason for these things. Now he was very curious.

Why had not his father told him the old truths of the Ancient Ones? Perhaps it was simply that his father did not think it important. After all, Haske had never before in his life made a bear angry. He had seen only a few bears and they had run from him. But now he must ask his father about these things.

Riding Woman and Desbah came out of the house, and his mother said, "Our supper is ready. Come, let us eat. I shall keep the food warm for your father and Many Goats."

Old Grandfather woke up, and Riding Woman gave him food. Desbah lay down by the old man and went to sleep.

It was dark before Night Singer and Many Goats returned with the water from the spring. The wagon stopped before the hogan, and Night Singer called, "Haske! I have something here for you. Come and see."

When Haske looked into the wagon-bed he saw Gray Eyes! She wagged her tail and tried to sit up.

Riding Woman and Desbah, who was now awake, came running too. Desbah tried to climb into the

wagon in her joy, but Night Singer said, "No, Desbah. We must be careful with her. She has some broken ribs, and she is very weak. She was dragging herself along the trail, trying to reach home. We picked her up. With good care and food she will be all right in a week or so."

Riding Woman lifted Gray Eyes gently and laid her on a soft blanket in the wagon shed. Ute came, crying softly, and lay down near his companion. Haske brought food and water and placed them nearby.

After the men had eaten supper, Many Goats took his blanket and spread it on the ground by the corral. Here he would sleep. Night Singer and

Haske sat near the hogan door and watched a big orange moon roll on the edge of the desert before it sailed off into the sky.

"Is it true, my father, that the spirits of our ancestors live in the bears?" Haske asked.

Night Singer answered, "That is what the Ancient Ones tell us, my son. The old people will continue to believe it. But you and I need not follow their beliefs."

"But we do not kill the bears," said Haske. "And we do not eat the meat. White hunters do these things. Store Sitter hunts the bear every fall, and he eats the meat. If we do not believe as the Old Ones do, why don't we have bear meat to eat when the hunger months come?"

Night Singer answered his son thoughtfully: "We must respect the feelings of others even though we do not agree with them. Out of respect for the Old Ones we do not kill the bear or eat his meat. But we must not let the Old Ones hold us back. We must progress with time. On the other hand, we must not push them and try to make them agree with our beliefs. But just between us, my son, do not worry. A bear is only a bear."

Quietly they went into the hogan and went to bed. Tomorrow would be a busy day.

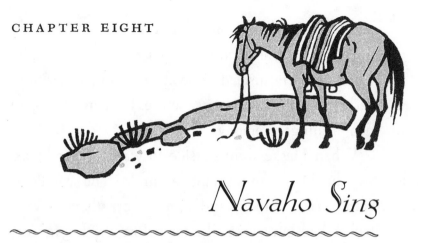

# CHAPTER EIGHT

# Navaho Sing

BEFORE SUNUP next morning Haske was awakened by noises. Already Navahos were arriving in wagons and on horseback for the Sing. Some of the people had traveled all night.

A Navaho Sing is a ceremony for making a sick person well. A Medicine Man is one who knows all plants and herbs, and makes medicine from them. He also communes with the Navaho gods and is respected for his powers of healing. There are different songs for different sicknesses. One who knows these songs, and the proper way to sing them, must lead the singing.

Sand paintings are made by certain men who know the sacred symbols. Different symbols are used for different sicknesses and injuries. These paintings are made of colored sand and must be perfect. If a sand painting is not made exactly right, it will do harm instead of good. A sand painter must study and train for years before he may take part in a healing ceremony.

When Haske went outside to wash up for breakfast, he saw many people around. The Medicine Man, Wind Talker, and others were there. Wind Talker had built a small altar before the hogan door and placed on it his medicine bowls, feathers, and buckskin bags. These would be used in the ceremony to heal Old Grandfather.

Haske ate hurriedly and walked over to the hogan door, where he stood watching the two sand painters inside. They were squatting on their heels, pouring dry colors between their thumbs and forefingers. They were making beautiful symbols. There were painted symbols of corn, squash, and lightning. There was a painting of a bear and a horned toad. Many circles and figures were drawn in bright colors. Around three sides of the painting was a brilliant rainbow. While he watched, the men finished the sand painting and for a few minutes they studied it carefully. Then they moved toward the door.

Haske pressed his body against the wall so the men would not notice him. His heart was pounding with excitement. He had felt an inspiration while he watched the men painting with sand. Now for the first time in his life he knew what he wanted to be when he grew up. He wanted to be a sand painter. How thrilling it would be to feel the colored sand pour between his fingers! How thrilling it would be to feel the magic flow through his hands! Magic so great that only the gods could understand it! He must speak to his father about this, and discuss it with Old Grandfather.

At last everything was ready for the ceremony. People began to enter the hogan. They sat on each side of the sand painting, backs against the walls. Haske sat down between his father and his uncle, Many Goats. The men sat on one side. The women sat on the opposite side. Haske saw his mother among the women. She held Desbah on her lap.

Slowly through the door came Old Grandfather. Ben Turquoise helped him in and guided him to the sand painting. The old man wore only a loincloth. His long gray hair hung over his shoulders. Carefully he sat down in the center of the sand painting, crossed his legs, and waited.

The song leader began a chant, soft at first, but growing louder. Now the people joined in, and the voices blended. The leader held a gourd-rattle and shook it violently. The hogan seemed to breathe the song. It did not sound like the voices of many people. It sounded like one great voice with many intonations. Haske felt strange. He said within himself, "It is good. It is beautiful. I am in my mother's hogan, and there is no world outside. There is no day or night or yesterday or tomorrow. It is all here and now." He closed his eyes and swayed with the rhythm about him.

Now Wind Talker moved over to Old Grandfather. The old man sat very still. He closed his eyes. Wind Talker began painting symbols around the wounds on chest, face, and forehead. He sprinkled the wounds with blessed cornmeal and the yellow pollen of wild plants. He touched Old

Grandfather's chest and head with an eagle's feather. Then he pointed the feather to the East, the West, the North, and the South. Finally he gave the old man a drink from each of the altar bowls. Then with great dignity the Medicine Man left the hogan. The ceremony was over.

The people waited until Old Grandfather was helped outside. After everyone had left the hogan, the sand painters returned and erased the sacred painting. A sand painting must always be erased before sundown.

Wind Talker put all of his medicine bowls, buckskin bags, and feathers away and removed the altar. Then he rolled a cigarette and sat down to talk with the other men. Now that the ceremony was over everyone was at ease. Women laughed and talked as they cooked supper. Children played and ran races. Men fed their horses and talked of many things.

Before Wind Talker rode away after supper, Riding Woman gave him a beautiful woven blanket and two heavy silver bracelets. These were gifts of gratitude in return for restoring Old Grandfather to health.

# CHAPTER NINE

# A Paper from Washington

ONE MORNING early in September a yellow bus stopped at the hogan. The driver was Jim Willie, a Navaho man. Haske was not happy to see the bus. During the previous year he had attended the Mountain Day School for six months. He had not been able to go during December, January, and February because of heavy snows and bad roads. Because of this he had fallen behind in his work and did not want to go back to school. Besides, he did not like sitting inside a room for long hours. He felt cooped up and restless. It was much more fun to be outside where one felt free.

[ 51 ]

He did remember a few nice things about the school. He had learned to speak some English, and had even learned to read in a book the teacher gave him. There were beautiful bright pictures in another book which he liked to look at. He remembered the good hot lunches, too, and the many toys to play with. But perhaps best of all he liked the smooth paper and the pencil which the teacher gave to each student. How easy it was to make beautiful sketches when he had such things to work with. A part of each day the teacher had let them draw.

Jim Willie held a paper in his hand as he talked with Riding Woman. He told her what the paper meant. It was from Washington and must be obeyed.

"Every child of school age must attend school," he said.

That night when his father came home, they told him about the paper from Washington.

Night Singer said, "It is good! I want my children to have an education. Haske must study hard and learn much. When Desbah is old enough, she must go to school and learn from books. The old way of life for the Navaho is going fast. We must learn new ways."

On Saturday morning Riding Woman said, "Haske must have new clothing for school. Today we shall go to the Trading Post."

She took a rug which she had woven and folded it neatly. Night Singer brought from the shed the last of the spring shearing. He lifted the big bag of wool and put it in the wagon. The horses were hitched to the wagon and stood waiting.

As Riding Woman buttoned Desbah's velvet blouse, she said, "Old Grandfather, won't you come with us? You are well now, and the ride will do you good. Come with us, and I shall buy you something."

Haske leaned against Old Grandfather's knee and said, "Please do come with us. You may sit on the bag of soft wool and tell me stories."

But the old man shook his head and said he would not go. There was something he wanted to do, but he would not tell Haske what it was.

The rest of the family climbed into the wagon. Riding Woman and Desbah sat in the bed of the wagon. Night Singer and Haske sat on the driver's seat. The horses pulled, the wheels rolled, and they were off. Ute and Gray Eyes followed behind. Both dogs were well and strong again. They loved to follow the wagon wherever it went.

After a two-hour ride they came to the Trading Post. It was a large rock building. Around it were

cedar trees and clumps of tumbleweed. In front was
a long hitching rail. A dozen Navahos were sitting
under the trees eating their lunch.

Night Singer tied the horses to the hitching rail
and stopped to speak with friends. Riding Woman
took her rug and went with Haske and Desbah into
the store. When they got inside, they saw many
other Navahos. It is not polite for a Navaho to
rush into a store and begin trading at once. Riding

Woman shook hands with her friends. Then she drew Haske and Desbah to a corner, and they sat down.

There was so much to see and admire! Haske looked about the room. He saw new saddles hung against the walls, and cowboy boots and large western hats. He saw crisp new Levis and bright shirts. Printed calico and bright velvet. Handsome, heavy silver jewelry hung behind the counter. Riding Woman told him that some of the silver belts, necklaces, and bracelets were over a hundred years old. On the other side of the room Haske saw long rows of canned peaches, apricots, and corn. Large sacks of flour, pinto beans, sugar, and cornmeal were heaped against one wall. There was candy, too, and chewing gum in a glass case on the counter.

After a few minutes Riding Woman stood up and walked slowly to the counter. Store Sitter smiled and spoke to her. They began trading for the things she wanted. Store Sitter liked the rug which Riding Woman had brought. He said he would allow her twenty dollars in trade for it. While they were trading, Night Singer brought in the big bag of wool. Store Sitter weighed the wool on his large scales. Haske did not hear what Store Sitter said

the wool was worth, but he saw his father smile. This meant it had brought a good price.

After Riding Woman and Night Singer had finished their trading, it was time for lunch. They found a nice shady spot under a tree and sat down. Riding Woman took out of a brown paper bag some of the food she had traded for. There were canned peaches, canned tomatoes, dried beef, a big loaf of store-bread, and strawberry soda pop. How good it tasted!

When Haske had finished his lunch, he walked to the corral behind the store. He must visit Night Wind before he went home. The black horse neighed a friendly greeting and trotted to the gate. Haske put his arms around the sleek neck. The horse rubbed his velvet nose against Haske's shoulder.

Haske said, "I don't know when I can come back again. I've got to go to school every day and learn new things. But I won't forget you. When I come again, I shall ask Store Sitter if I may ride on your back. We shall spend a whole day together, just you and me. Good-bye, Night Wind."

The sun was in the western sky and the shadows were growing long. The family told their friends good-bye and climbed into the wagon for the trip home. Haske saw many packages and wondered what was in each. Night Singer took from his pocket a bag of candy and passed it to each of them. No one talked. It was nice just to ride along together and feel happiness inside.

Ute and Gray Eyes rode in the wagon all the way home. Haske gave each of them a bite of candy. He saved two pieces for Old Grandfather.

It was getting dark when they reached home. Riding Woman went into the hogan and lighted the oil lamp. Desbah was with her mother. Haske went with Night Singer to put the horses in the corral and feed them.

When Haske and his father came into the hogan, Riding Woman said, "Old Grandfather has gone away. He is not here."

Desbah was crying, and Haske felt very bad. He closed his eyes and would not cry, but the happiness had gone away. He kept thinking about Old Grandfather wandering alone in the darkness. Where would he go? What would he eat? How Haske wished he might run out to find the Old One and bring him home. But Night Singer said, "Old Grandfather does what he thinks is best. We must not shame him by treating him as a child. He will come back when he is ready."

Riding Woman knew how her son felt. She walked over to him, put her arms about his shoulders, and said, "My son, do not worry about the Old One. He has food with him. He took the bread left from breakfast and the dried meat. He has plenty to eat, and he will come back soon."

Both Haske and Desbah felt better at their mother's words. So they opened all the packages. There were new brown shoes, a warm red shirt, a pair of blue Levis, and a heavy blue jacket for Haske. There was a pair of black shoes for Desbah. There were yards of bright velvet and calico for both Desbah and her mother. Even Night Singer had a warm new jacket and Levis. He also had bought some blocks of silver with which to make Indian jewelry. There was enough food to last the family for several weeks.

Surely Old Grandfather would soon be back and everything would be all right.

# CHAPTER TEN

# Back to School

EARLY on Monday morning Haske dressed, ate breakfast, and waited by the door for the school bus. Desbah wanted to go with him, but she was too young. Riding Woman told her that in two more years she could go to school. Gray Eyes and Ute had already gone with Night Singer to herd the sheep. How Haske wished he were with them!

The bus rattled up. A loud blast from the horn made Desbah jump. Haske hurried out and climbed in. Away they went, bouncing over the road. There were many other boys and girls in the bus. As they bumped over rough places, they laughed at the way they bounced around.

Jim Willie said, "Boys and girls, do you know what I call this bus? I call it *The Bronco,* because it's so rough. It's like a bucking horse."

Everyone liked the name Jim Willie gave to the bus, and they repeated it over and over again so they would not forget it. They, too, would call it *The Bronco.*

When they reached the schoolhouse, Haske saw a strange woman. She had not been there the year before. Jim Willie said, "Children, this is your new teacher, Miss Smith."

Miss Smith helped everyone to choose a seat. Then she told them how happy she was to be teaching Navaho boys and girls. She wanted them to be happy at school. She asked them what they liked best to do.

Each one wanted to tell about the thing he liked best to do. Haske said he liked to draw pictures. Miss Smith said she liked to read poetry and promised to read some poems to them. By lunch time everyone was well acquainted with everyone else. No one felt shy or frightened. Haske was actually glad to be back in school.

Jim Willie's wife, Ellen, cooked lunch for the school children. She was a jolly woman and always kind. She taught them good table manners. How to sit straight at the table. How to use their knives, forks, and spoons properly. She always set the table with care to make it look pretty. Lunch time was a happy time, and there was much good food.

In the afternoon everyone read aloud for the teacher. Haske remembered most of the English words he had learned. He read well. He looked at all the bright pictures in his new book. They interested him, and he hoped that someday he might paint pictures like these.

Haske was happy to find smooth white paper and a bright red pencil on his desk. He picked up the pencil. It had a beautiful sharp point. Just to hold it in his fingers made him joyful. How he wished the teacher would let him draw a picture!

Then Miss Smith said, just as if she knew what Haske was thinking, "This paper is not for drawing. See the ruled lines? Please do not draw on this paper. It is to be used for your writing lessons."

Haske's gladness went out of him. He laid the pencil down and blinked his eyes to hold back tears of disappointment.

Miss Smith now held before them a large sheet of heavy paper and said, "This is the paper we shall use for drawing. See, it has no ruled lines. On Mondays, Wednesdays, and Fridays we shall use one hour for drawing and painting. I shall pass paper, crayons, and boxes of watercolors to each of you. I shall expect you to make some nice pictures."

As the children rode home on *The Bronco* after school, they sang a song. It was the Happiness Song of the Navaho people. Haske sang loudest of all.

# CHAPTER ELEVEN

# *The Storm*

LATE ONE EVENING in November Old Grandfather returned. He came in just before dark. He had been gone a long time, but now it was cold and he needed shelter.

"A big storm is coming," he said. "I can smell it in the wind."

Sure enough, the storm came in the night. By morning everything was covered with snow.

The school bus could not travel over the roads because of the deep snow. Haske liked school, but he was glad to be home with Old Grandfather. He wondered how the old man could smell the coming storm. Only the very wise could do that.

All morning Riding Woman and Night Singer melted snow for water. They had built a fire near the corral and set big buckets of snow over it. They were glad the storm had come, because now there would be plenty of water for the family. There would be plenty for the horses and sheep too.

After Haske had carried water to the sheep, he went into his mother's hogan. He sat down by Old

Grandfather and told him about the paintings he made at school. Then he said, "You are very wise and very old. I want you to help me, Old Grandfather. I want you to help me become a sand painter. Tell me what I must do. After you tell me, I shall speak to my mother and father."

The old man thought for a while before he answered. Presently he said, "To become a sand painter, you must become a singer. This will require many years of study in the Navaho religion and medicine. You will have to live and work with one who knows these things."

Haske put another stick of wood in the fire pit before he said, "When school is out in the spring, I shall have all summer to learn these things. I shall tell my parents what I want to be when I grow up."

Old Grandfather leaned forward and touched Haske's arm. In a whisper he said, "My grandson, you will have to give up the white man's school. You cannot follow the two trails at the same time. The Indian trail goes one way. The white man's trail goes another. You will have to decide which of the two ways you will follow." These words troubled Haske deeply.

Riding Woman came in and cooked potatoes and tortillas for lunch. They had no meat. No more sheep should be butchered at this time. They would have to wait awhile before they killed another sheep. Riding Woman must save as many sheep as possible for baby lambs and wool. Always the winter months, especially January and February, brought hunger to the Navaho people. These months were called Hunger Days, for all the food stored in the fall had been eaten by then.

After lunch Night Singer said, "For supper maybe we shall have meat! I'm going rabbit hunting. In a snow such as this I should be able to get a rabbit. Haske, do you want to come with me?"

Haske liked to go to the mountains with his father. So he quickly dressed in his warmest clothing and followed Night Singer out of the hogan.

# CHAPTER TWELVE

# The Hunt

~~~~~~~~~~~~~~~~~~~~~~~~~~~~~~~~~~~~~~~~

HASKE and his father climbed past the foothills. Up, up they went into the mountains. Here heavy brush and trees grew. This was wild country, cold and still. The big pines drooped under their load of snow.

Suddenly Night Singer stopped and listened. Haske hardly breathed for fear of making a noise. Everything was silent except for an occasional plop-plop as snow fell from the trees.

They were about to walk on when they heard a crash in the snow-heavy brush and a great buck deer went hurtling through the woods!

Haske was excited. He saw his father raise the gun to his shoulder, take careful aim, and fire. The big buck seemed to leap into the air, then fall. Noise from the gun had deafened Haske for a second or two. Now everything was quiet again. He could hardly believe that so much had happened in such a short time.

Haske ran to overtake his father, but Night Singer had reached the deer and stood looking down at it

by the time Haske arrived. Night Singer plunged his hunting knife into the deer's throat so the blood would spill and the meat would be good for eating.

Handing the rifle to Haske, he said, "You wait here and guard the deer. Coyotes may come around. I shall be back as soon as possible with my horse."

Haske's father had taught him to be careful with the rifle. He had also taught him how to shoot well if he needed to do so.

As he waited for his father's return, he wished that Gray Eyes and Ute had been allowed to come along. How nice it would be to have them with him now! But Night Singer would never let the dogs go

hunting with him. When he was only a boy, he had owned a dog which he loved very much. On a rabbit hunt the dog had got in the line of fire and been shot. After that, he would never take a dog to hunt rabbits.

Once Haske heard a small noise behind him. Turning quickly, he saw a rabbit struggling through the deep snow. It could not travel fast, and it would have been so easy to kill it. He looked at the deer and thought of all the meat they had now. They would not go hungry. They no longer needed rabbit meat for food, so he let the rabbit live.

At last Haske heard his father riding up the mountain, singing. Together they lifted the body of the deer and swung it across the horse's back. They tied it securely, so it would not slip off, and started for home.

After they reached home, the deer was quickly skinned. Venison steaks were fried and hot biscuits made. Before he went to sleep that night, Haske thought how good the storm had been to them. Because of it, Old Grandfather had come back to them, the sheep and horses had a big tank of drinking water, and the family had fresh meat to eat.

On the following morning Riding Woman said, "Today I shall make jerky. If we want the meat to keep for a while without spoiling, I must begin drying it today."

With her sharpest knife she began cutting the meat into long thin strips. She worked fast because she had learned how to do this many years ago. Often, when a sheep was butchered for the family, she dried some of the meat. She had learned just how thin to slice it and how to cut away the fat.

After all the meat was cut up, Riding Woman placed it in a large tub and carried it outside to the drying pole. This was a long slender pole laid across two forked posts. The ends of the pole rested securely in the forked ends of the stout posts. Over the pole she carefully hung the long strips of venison for the sun and air to dry. Gray Eyes and Ute would guard the meat from marauding animals. They had been trained never to bother meat on the drying pole.

After a few days the meat would be dry and crisp. Then Riding Woman would take it down, pack it in clean flour sacks, and hang it against the hogan walls. When the family wanted dried meat for dinner, she would boil some of it with potatoes, and it would taste delicious. The dried meat, or jerky, could also be carried on long trips without being cooked.

# CHAPTER THIRTEEN

# Best of the Old, Best of the New

OLD GRANDFATHER stayed with the family three weeks. Haske had many long talks with him about becoming a sand painter. The old man loved Haske very much and wanted him to have a good life and to be happy.

One day he said to him, "My grandson, you do not know what is best. You hear my words, but there is fear in your heart. The white man's teaching is making you sick. Already it has a power over you. It is a bad thing to mock the gods. Navaho gods are powerful and will send evil to those who turn from them. When you choose the white man's trail, you offend the Navaho gods."

Haske was frightened at Old Grandfather's words. He had heard stories of what happened to those who offended the powerful gods. They had grown ill and dried up just as a hot wind dries the green corn. Even the Medicine Man could not help them.

Haske felt a chill run down his back and he thought, "I really *am* sick. It is true that the fear in my heart has the power to make me sick." Aloud he asked, "What shall I do, Old Grandfather? I did not mean to offend the Navaho gods. Please tell me quickly, what must I do?"

The old man had dozed off to sleep. Haske shook his shoulder and repeated the question: "Please tell me, what must I do now?"

The old man opened his eyes and tried to remember what they had been talking about. After a moment he said, "I am an old man. Sometimes I cannot think clearly. I cannot tell you what you must do. If you want to know, go to the top of the Sacred Mountain. Take no food. Fast for four days and four nights and ask the gods to show you what you must do. They will set your feet upon the right trail, a trail of beauty."

Haske said, "Thank you, Old Grandfather," but the old man did not hear. He had dozed off again.

That same evening Haske went with Night Singer to feed the horses. While he was alone with his father, Haske said, "Tomorrow I shall not be here when the school bus comes for me. Will you ask Jim Willie to tell Miss Smith that I shall not be in school for four days?"

Night Singer stared at Haske with wide eyes. He knew nothing about the talks his son had with Old Grandfather. He did not even know that the boy wanted to become a sand painter.

Haske had not yet spoken about it to his parents. He had hoped that he would not have to tell them now. He wanted to wait until he had fasted for four days on Sacred Mountain. After the gods had spoken to him, he would know what to say to his mother and father.

Night Singer bluntly asked, "Where do you expect to be when the school bus comes in the morning? Why won't you be in school for four days?"

Suddenly Haske felt trapped. It would be hard to make his father understand. Lifting his head and squaring his shoulders, he looked straight into the eyes of Night Singer and said, "I must go to Sacred Mountain and fast for four days. I have offended the Navaho gods."

For a while Night Singer was silent. He looked both angry and sad. Finally he asked, "What have you done, my son, to offend the Navaho gods? Who told you to go to Sacred Mountain and fast?"

"Old Grandfather told me these things," answered Haske. "You see, Father, I want to become a sand painter. I must choose between the white man's trail and the Navaho trail. Old Grandfather said the gods will tell me which trail I must follow."

Haske did not feel that he had betrayed Old Grandfather. He felt that Night Singer would know the wisdom of the old man's advice.

But his father's next words struck him like a blow. Haske felt sick when Night Singer said, "There will be no more such talk in our hogan! The Old One will be forbidden to speak of such things." Then he added in a kinder tone, "My son, you have not offended our gods. You are young and do not realize that Old Grandfather lives in the past. You must go to school every day and learn the new ways. The world is changing very fast and we must change with it."

Haske felt that a rope was tied to either arm and that he was being pulled both ways at once. When he went to bed, he could not sleep for thinking and worrying. All sorts of thoughts raced in his head. There seemed to be two different worlds, and he liked both of them. Only after he had made up his mind that he would continue going to school, did he fall asleep at last.

The following afternoon, when Haske got home from school, he learned that Grandfather had left. No one was home except his mother and Desbah. Night Singer had gone to a Sing for a sick friend. He would not return that night. Haske knew all was not right. He knew that his father had spoken to Old Grandfather and that the Old One had gone away feeling unwanted.

At supper Riding Woman saw that Haske was not eating his food. By the light of the center fire she saw that her son was troubled, and she understood how he felt.

Finally she said, "Your father told me all about it, my son. This morning he spoke to the Old One and tried to explain that school is good. But Old Grandfather could not understand. He was hurt and offended. He left without saying good-bye."

Haske did not try to hide his tears. He kept his eyes on his mother's face. For the first time in his life he saw the strength and courage in her face. Until now he had seen only the beauty and tenderness. Suddenly he was ashamed of his tears. He stopped crying and smiled at his mother.

Riding Woman said, "Now you feel better and must eat your supper."

She put hot food on his plate and warmed his coffee. While Haske ate hungrily, his mother explained all the things he needed to know.

She said, "My son, you have made an anthill look like a mountain. You have worried about which trail to follow. There is only one trail. You have come to believe that some things are all good and some things are all bad. This is not true. The Indian and the white man are not so different as you might think. Both have the same needs, and each must try to understand the other. This is why school is so important. At school you learn the white man's language. You cannot understand another person until you can talk with him. By speaking with others you learn what they are thinking and how they feel. This brings understanding between people."

Riding Woman saw that Desbah had gone to sleep by the fire. She picked up the little girl and wrapped a blanket about her. Then she tucked Desbah into her sheepskin bed and sat down again beside Haske.

"So you see, my son, there is only one trail," she continued. "Follow it and keep the best of the old ways while learning the best of the new ways."

Haske felt very happy. His mother had made him understand, and he no longer felt that he was being pulled in two directions. She had set his feet upon the trail as surely as the Navaho gods could have done. And he would make it a trail of beauty.

# CHAPTER FOURTEEN

# A Christmas Present

Now IT WOULD soon be Christmas. Haske liked school so much he was sorry about the Christmas vacation. He would not have minded a day or even two, but the vacation lasted a whole week! He would miss reading exciting stories in the books at school. He would miss using the drawing paper and bright watercolors. He knew that he would be a little lonely.

It wasn't that he wouldn't enjoy his family. Oh, he would! But he wished Old Grandfather might be with them. Haske wanted to explain to the old man that Night Singer did not mean to offend him. He also wanted to tell Old Grandfather that school is a good thing, that it would not make a Navaho forget the ways of his people.

Even in school Haske could not forget Old Grandfather. During the drawing period on Monday, he remembered the story which the old man had told him about the Kiowas and Comanches. Thoughtfully he began to sketch the things he remembered. Old Grandfather had told the story so well that every detail was vivid. Haske forgot those around him. He forgot that he was in school, that the clock was ticking away the minutes. It was as if he and Old Grandfather were on the mountain. Together they fought the Kiowas and Comanches and

chased them off the high bluff. His pencil recorded the details of the battle.

When the picture was finished, Haske knew it was the best work he had ever done. How he wished Old Grandfather could see it! He knew this could never be, for the old man's eyes were almost blind. But he knew, too, that Old Grandfather would always remember that battle. He did not need the picture. Haske put the painting in his desk.

On Friday afternoon Miss Smith asked them all to go into the dining room. This was a surprise! Cookies and hot chocolate awaited them. By each plate was a beautifully wrapped package such as Haske had never seen before.

Miss Smith said, "You all know that tomorrow our Christmas vacation begins. You each have a small gift beside your plate. Take these home with you, and have a happy Christmas."

After the party they all returned to the classroom to get ready to leave. Several of the children took things from their desks and gave them to the teacher. The presents were not wrapped and everyone could see them. One of the girls gave a small Navaho rug, a new one with red and black stripes. Another gave a beautiful silver bracelet. Two of the boys gave silver rings with turquoise stones in them. Each one said, "Merry Christmas," as the present was given.

The teacher was surprised. She had not seen the children bring the presents. They had hidden them under their coats and in their pockets when they had come to school in the morning. She thanked them in a way that made their eyes shine with happiness. But she told them that they should not have brought such beautiful gifts.

Haske sat very still. This was his first Christmas at school, and he had brought nothing to give to his teacher. He felt very bad about it until suddenly he knew what he would do.

As the children left the room to get on the bus, Haske took his painting with him. When he passed the teacher's desk, he handed it to her saying, "Merry Christmas! I want to give it to you." Then he ran through the door like a small deer.

# CHAPTER FIFTEEN

# A Beautiful Way to Go

~~~~~~~~~~~~~~~~~~~~~~~~~~~~~~~~~~~~~~~~~~~~~

SPRING CAME EARLY. The days were longer now. When Haske came home from school, he chopped wood or helped in other ways. Sometimes he played with Desbah, teaching her words in English.

Only once since last fall had Haske seen the black horse, Night Wind. How he longed to see him again! He had done so many paintings of Night Wind that Miss Smith said, "Haske, you paint the same horse often. Is this your horse?" There were several paintings of Night Wind on the walls of his hogan too. His parents were very proud of their son's paintings.

One evening that spring, just as the family sat
down to supper, Old Grandfather came back. He
looked older and very tired. He ate a little bread
and drank some coffee before he slept. The next
morning he would eat no breakfast. He asked only
that Haske walk with him to the foothills. He
wanted to spend the day in the warm sunshine,
resting. Riding Woman put some bread and meat
into a bag for his lunch, and he thanked her.

Taking the old man's arm, Haske guided him to
the foothills. Here the juniper and cedar trees grew
and birds sang. The winds were warm and gentle.
Haske found a sheltered spot on the hillside and
helped Old Grandfather to lie down.

The old man said, "Thank you, my grandson. You are a good boy. You must hurry back to your mother's hogan now."

Haske did not like to leave him there all alone. He knew Old Grandfather was sick and that he did not want to be a bother to anyone. Haske let the tears run down his face as he looked at the frail, lonely old man.

He sat down beside him and touched Old Grandfather's face, saying, "After school I shall come and help you back to my mother's hogan. I shall be thinking of you all day."

The Old One said, "No, do not come for me, my grandson. I shall not be here. I must go. Someone is coming for me, and I want to go. Listen to my song, and you will understand." Faintly Old Grandfather sang his song:

"From the high summit of the Sacred Mountain
The young warrior gods come for my sake.
From the top of the black mountains
Nayenezgani comes for my sake.
Over the white ridges of the foothills
Tobadsistsini comes for my sake.
In the center they meet.
Near the Place of Emergence
They meet for my sake.
Although the smooth winds guard the door
The slayer of enemy gods opens the way."

Haske knew this was a song sung only by one about to die. He cried, "No, no, no! I shall come for you, and you will go back to my mother's hogan."

At school Haske thought of Old Grandfather all day. He did not want to play. He did not want to eat. He could hardly wait for Jim Willie to take him home.

As soon as he climbed off the school bus, Haske said to his mother, "I must go to see about Old

Grandfather first. I am sure that he needs me. I'll chop some wood when I get back."

Desbah wanted to go with him, so together they ran to the foothills. Desbah had to run very fast to keep up.

Haske hurried around the hillside and stopped. Old Grandfather was not there! He ran to other small hills calling to Old Grandfather, but no answer came. The children searched until almost dark, but Old Grandfather had gone away. Even his tin cup was gone.

Once more Haske called, then stood quietly listening. From high above, only his echo "Old Grandfather" came back and the echo did not sound like Haske's voice. This frightened Desbah, and slowly the children returned home.

Riding Woman asked no questions when they came back alone. She understood. Night Singer returned from herding the sheep. No one felt like eating supper. Riding Woman held Desbah on her lap and looked only at the dying cook-fire. Night Singer sat under the cedar tree and smoked.

Haske could stand the silence no longer. He felt he would die if he did not say something.

"Old Grandfather has gone," he said.

Riding Woman just nodded her head and kept looking at the fire.

Night Singer answered him, "Yes, he has gone away. He had waited a very long time, and he wanted to go."

Haske felt a little better at these kind words. Then he asked, "But *how* did he go? He could not walk well alone. I know that we shall not see him again, but I do not know how he went. He could not walk far without help."

Night Singer looked at Riding Woman. His mother just sat there holding tight to Desbah. Haske thought, "My mother feels the same pain that I feel. She loved Old Grandfather and cannot talk about it."

Night Singer said, "My son, it is that way with the Old Ones. They do not die like younger people. The Ancient Ones, people who have been gone for a long time, come for them. They came for Old Grandfather. They helped him to go. He took the tin cup so that he might drink from the cold springs along the way. Do not feel sad."

Haske was grateful to his father for his explanation. He thought about it and said, "That is a beautiful way to go. Maybe Old Grandfather's eyes are strong again. Maybe the Cloud People took him right over the mountains. Old Grandfather would love that!"

Haske was glad now that he had not told Old Grandfather about his decision. He had not had a chance to tell him that he wanted to continue school, that he had changed his mind about wanting to be a singer and sand painter. He knew that it would have disappointed Old Grandfather.

That night after the family had gone to bed, the owl returned to the cedar tree. Before anyone could get through the door, the owl spoke three times!

Haske lay still and thought about many things. He thought about the owl and wondered why it had spoken to his family. He thought about the cedar tree near their door and wondered why the owl always perched in its branches. He thought about Old Grandfather and his belief that owls brought bad messages to the people. He thought about his parents and wondered why they did not believe in such things. Finally he stopped wondering and went to sleep.

# CHAPTER SIXTEEN

# The Owl's Message

THE END of the school term had come quickly. Haske now herded the sheep daily with the dogs. Sometimes Desbah went along to play with the small lambs. It was fun to spend his days in the open again.

One morning Haske awoke to the sound of rain on the roof. He lay on his blanket and saw Dawn Woman come slowly across the desert. Today she brought a pale gray light to the world. Raindrops, silver and cool, fell from her fingers. Haske felt the damp air on his face and thought about the black horse. How he would love to ride Night Wind on such a day as this!

Outside he heard the jingle of harness. Night Singer and Riding Woman were hitching the horses to the wagon, which was loaded with logs. He remembered now that his parents were going to the Trading Post today.

He wished he might go with them so he could visit Night Wind. He knew the black horse would be happy to see him again. But his father was taking the load of logs to Store Sitter. There would be no space in the wagon for the two children. Haske and Desbah must stay home today.

Riding Woman came in and said, "Get up, little lazy ones. Your father and I are ready to leave."

Haske jumped up and ran to the door. He held his brown hands out for the rain to wash them. He cupped his fingers, catching rain, and washed his face.

His mother drew her shawl over her shoulders and said, "I left your breakfast in the pan by the fire. Take care of your little sister. We shall be home before it is late." Climbing onto the seat beside Night Singer, she waved to them. The wagon creaked and rumbled away.

Haske and Desbah stood in the doorway and watched their parents ride away. Ute and Gray

Eyes watched too. The dogs wanted to follow the wagon, but Night Singer told them to stay and guard the children.

Turning to Desbah, Haske said, "I know what we shall do! I shall draw and paint a picture, and you may watch. After I have finished my painting, I will let you make one of your own with my paints. Would you like that?"

Both children were glad that the teacher had given Haske paper, pencils, and a box of watercolors. When school was out, all the students brought home some of the things they wanted. No longer did Haske have to draw pictures in the sand and slowly erase them as the shadows grew long across the desert.

Now he lay on his stomach and sketched the figure of a horse. Desbah lay beside him and watched. She did not know that the horse was Night Wind. Nor did she know that the boy riding the horse was her own brother. Only Haske knew these things, and he would not tell.

The dogs lay by the door, but they did not sleep. With a low growl Ute sat up. His ears were pointed forward, listening. Gray Eyes moved outside, and suddenly both dogs barked.

Remembering the owl, Haske jumped up and looked out. He heard the sound of a motor and was frightened. Navahos drove only wagons over this road. The school bus would not be running after school was out. Who could be coming to his mother's hogan? Why would anyone drive through the rain when the roads were so bad?

Haske thought of the tales he had heard and grew more frightened. Evil spirits sometimes took strange forms and carried children away. Their parents never saw them again. Desbah had come and put her arm around her brother. He felt her shiver with fear as they stood silently watching while the noise grew louder and came nearer and nearer.

Around the bend in the road from behind the foothills a car came slowly. It was a blue car. Haske thought he had seen it somewhere before, but he was not sure. Ute and Gray Eyes moved forward, and the hair on their backs stood up. The car came slowly toward the hogan. Through the mist and rain Haske could not see the driver.

He told Desbah to hide behind the sheepskins. He told her not to cry or make any noise. He would meet the stranger and take care of everything.

While he watched, Haske saw an arm wave in a friendly manner and someone called, "Hello." Haske knew the voice. It was Miss Smith's voice. He told Desbah to come out of hiding and spoke to the dogs, assuring them that it was a friend. He waved his arms and smiled broadly. Everything was all right now.

In a couple of minutes Miss Smith stopped her car and ran through the rain into the hogan. She was laughing and gay. Her first words were "Oh, Haske, I have good news for you!" She spoke to Desbah and asked where their parents were. When she learned that both Riding Woman and Night Singer were at the store, she said, "Then we shall go to the store. I have a check for you, and we must take care of it there."

Haske had never heard of such a thing as a check. He did not know what she was talking about. He remembered the owl and how it had spoken three times right before their door.

"What is a check, Miss Smith?" he asked. "Is it a bad message?"

Miss Smith laughed and answered, "No! This check is a very *good* message. Let's sit down while I tell you all about it."

Haske thought, "Then the owl brought a good message! I shall never again be afraid of owls."

Miss Smith sat down on the floor and crossed her feet like a Navaho. She asked Desbah to sit beside her, but the little girl did not know the teacher well, so she sat by Haske instead.

Miss Smith began by asking, "Do you remember the painting which you gave me for Christmas? It's because of the painting that I came today. A friend of mine works in a museum in New York. Each year in late spring the museum has an exhibit of children's paintings. The paintings are judged, and the best one is given a prize of one hundred dollars."

Miss Smith waited a moment, smiled, then said, "Haske, your painting won the prize! It was judged the best of all, and you will soon have a hundred dollars. So let's go to the store and tell your parents all about it and have the check cashed." She showed Haske the check with his own name on it.

He looked at the slip of paper. He touched his name with a brown finger and smiled. Suddenly his black brows came together in a frown as he asked, "But did you give my painting away?"

Miss Smith opened her eyes wide in hurt surprise and said, "Oh, Haske, I would never give away your beautiful painting! Of course I did not give it away. My friend who takes care of the exhibit will send the painting back to me very soon."

On their way to the store, as Miss Smith drove over the muddy road, she said, "Haske, would you mind telling me the story of the picture you gave me? It's so interesting. In it there is a very old man and a boy. They are standing on a high bluff overlooking the desert below. Down there, men are fighting and beautiful horses are rearing and running. I would like to know the story of it."

Haske sat very still for a moment. He half closed his eyes as he saw again in his mind each detail of the painting. Then he began softly, "That old man is my Old Grandfather. He told the story to me just as it really happened. That boy is me. I wanted to give the picture to Old Grandfather, but his eyes were almost blind and he could not see it."

Miss Smith felt that it hurt Haske to talk about this because he still missed Old Grandfather. She wanted to help him overcome his feeling of loneliness. She wanted him to learn to speak proudly of Old Grandfather without being hurt. So she said, "Haske, your grandfather was a wonderful story-teller. I know you are very proud of him. You are lucky to have had someone to tell you stories of the long ago. I think such a grandfather would be happy to know that his stories were loved and remembered. Why don't you do paintings of all the stories he told you? I think your grandfather would have liked that. Don't you?"

Haske had never thought of it in this way. Suddenly he smiled as he remembered how much Old Grandfather loved the old ways of his youth. Every time the old man spoke or told a story, he painted a picture with words. Haske thought, "Now I can keep the old ways which Old Grandfather loved so much by painting all the things he told me about. They will never change. That is better than being a sand painter."

To Miss Smith, aloud, he said, "Thank you," as she stopped her car in front of the Trading Post.

# CHAPTER SEVENTEEN

# Haske Sings
the Happiness Song

RIDING WOMAN AND NIGHT SINGER could hardly believe their eyes! They could not imagine why the teacher had brought Haske and Desbah to the store. Miss Smith sat in a corner of the Trading Post and slowly explained all about the painting, the exhibit, and the prize money. The parents did not understand English very well, so Store Sitter came over and interpreted for them. He spoke very correct Navaho. Haske listened carefully.

After a while Miss Smith took the paper again from her billfold. She asked Haske to sign his name across the back of the check. How glad he was that he had gone to school and learned to write his name! He signed the check with a pen which Store Sitter handed to him.

Store Sitter looked at the check and laughed loudly. He shook his head and slapped his leg. Then he called Haske to the counter and began stacking big round silver dollars in front of him. He asked Haske to count each dollar he put down. Haske counted and counted. Finally he reached one hundred!

Store Sitter said, "How are you going to carry all that money home?" Haske looked at his parents. They were smiling. He looked at Miss Smith and asked, "Is this really true? Are all of these dollars my very own?"

Miss Smith put an arm around his shoulders and said, "They all belong to you, Haske. Tell me what you want to buy with them."

Haske was overcome. There was something he wanted more than anything else in the whole world. Something that no one else knew about, but that was only a dream. He did not even dare think of it. He stood very still and felt hot tears squeeze through his lashes.

He remembered days when Desbah had cried from hunger. He thought about the beautiful jewelry his father could not make because he could not buy silver blocks. He thought how hard his mother worked to weave a rug to sell for food. He knew what he must do with his money.

He lifted his head and said, "I want to give it all to my parents. I want them to have it all."

Everyone was very quiet for a moment. Riding Woman spoke first. She spoke very softly in Navaho.

"My son is very generous and we thank you. But your father and I have spoken many times of buying a horse for you. You need a horse to ride when you herd my sheep. We first thought of this when Old Grandfather was hurt on the mountain. You needed a horse then. Now that you have money of your own, save it until we can find a horse to buy for you."

While his mother was speaking, Haske's black eyes began to shine and dance. Then suddenly he remembered that no one knew how he felt about the black horse which belonged to Store Sitter. If only his parents knew, maybe they would speak now of buying him. But maybe Store Sitter would not sell the black horse. Haske was afraid to ask, because if he could not have Night Wind now, he would lose him forever. He hesitated to ask, because he did not want to be refused before his parents and teacher.

With great dignity Haske asked Store Sitter to come outside with him. The trader followed him out into the rain. He wondered what the boy wanted. Just outside the door Haske stopped, looked straight into the man's eyes, and almost choked on the words as he said, "Please let me buy your black horse. I will give you all my dollars."

Store Sitter was very surprised. He said, "Why, I did not know you liked my horse so well. You've ridden him only once."

"But I have loved him for a long, long time. I always visit him when I come to the Trading Post. He knows me well. I gave him the name of Night

Wind and he knows his name. He is the only horse I want and I've wanted him for so long. If I cannot buy him now with all of this money, I can never have him."

Store Sitter heard the break in the boy's voice and understood how much the black horse meant to him.

"Let's go see what Night Wind thinks of the idea," he said and led the way to the corral.

The black horse saw Haske, tossed his head, and came trotting up to them. He nudged Haske's shoulder with his velvety nose, and Haske stroked his head gently.

"Well," said Store Sitter. "It does look as if Night Wind is on your side. All right, Haske, for seventy-five dollars you may have the horse. He is a little small for my weight, and I've thought of selling him for some time. Now I'm glad I kept him for you."

Haske was so happy he could not speak a word. He watched Store Sitter slip a bridle over the beautiful black head and buckle the strap. It was like a dream, and Haske wondered if he might wake up to find none of it true. Was Night Wind really to be his very own horse?

Store Sitter went into the stable and came back with a saddle which he put on the horse's back. After he had tightened and buckled the cinch, he said, "You might ask your mother to weave a nice saddle blanket for you. Now, here you are, Haske," and he handed the reins to the boy. "Take him to the hitching rail, then come into the store so we can get our business finished."

When Night Singer and Riding Woman learned that Haske had bought the fine horse which belonged to Store Sitter, they were pleased.

Haske counted out seventy-five dollars and gave them to Store Sitter. Then he pushed the rest of the silver dollars across the counter and said, "These are for the saddle and bridle."

Store Sitter smiled and shook his head, "Oh, no!" he said, "I want to trade the saddle and bridle for one of your paintings. I want you to paint a picture which I can hang in my store. Will you do that?" He pushed the dollars back across the counter.

Haske picked them up and said, "I'll paint two pictures for you. One for the saddle and one for the bridle."

Haske handed the rest of his money to his mother, saying, "I want you and my father to have this. Buy whatever you like, and please buy something nice for Desbah." Turning to Miss Smith, he said, "Thank you for everything."

Then he started out of the store, waving good-bye to Store Sitter as he left. He ran through the rain to where Night Wind waited for him. He lifted the reins and sprang into the saddle.

Night Wind made a soft, happy sound as Haske reached down and patted his sleek neck. Then, laying his ears back, he broke into a gallop as they started for home.

Haske looked around and saw his parents and Desbah following in the wagon. Night Singer had put the canvas cover over the wagon against the rain. But Haske liked the feel of the driving rain against his face and body, and he knew that Night Wind liked it too.

When he looked back a little later, the wagon was not in sight. He had left it far behind.

In his ears pounded the sound of his horse's hooves. His very own horse! There was a rhythm to that beat reminding him of something. All at once a smile curved his lips as, in time with his horse's hoof-beats, Haske began to sing the Navaho Happiness Song.